CN00353803

RUPERT

MEET ALL THESE FRIENDS IN BUZZ BOOKS:

Thomas the Tank Engine
The Animals of Farthing Wood
James Bond Junior
Fireman Sam
Joshua Jones
Rupert
Babar

First published in Great Britain 1993 by Buzz Books,
an imprint of Reed Children's Books
Michelin House, 81 Fulham Road, London, SW3 6RB
and Auckland, Melbourne, Singapore and Toronto

ISBN 1 85591 318 6

Printed in Italy by Olivotto

RUPERT™ and the CURIOUS CAR

Story by Norman Redfern
Illustrations by SPJ Design

"Eggs, tomatoes, carrots — now, what else do I need?" Mrs Bear was writing her shopping list. "Uncle Bruno's coming, so I had better buy plenty."

"Shall I do the shopping for you?" asked Rupert.

Mrs Bear was very pleased that Rupert was so thoughtful.

"I think that's everything," she said, picking up the list. "No, not quite!" and she added something at the end.

"I shan't be long," said Rupert, putting the shopping list in his trouser pocket.

Rupert set off for Mrs Fox's General Store in Nutwood. As he walked down the path, he saw someone strolling along in front of him. Rupert quickly caught him up.

"Hello, Doctor Lion," he said.

The doctor did not reply, but carried on walking, looking very serious.

"Are you feeling all right?" asked Rupert.

Doctor Lion looked at the little bear.

"I'm sorry, Rupert. I was miles away," he said. "Something very odd happened last night when I was visiting one of my patients. I can't understand it!"

"What happened?" asked Rupert.

"Edward Trunk had a tummy upset," said Doctor Lion, "so I jumped in the car and rushed round to see him. I was in such a hurry that I left the keys in the car."

"Oh, no," gasped Rupert. "Someone stole your car!"

"No, Rupert," replied Doctor Lion. "No one stole the car."

"Then what's wrong?" asked Rupert.

"When I went back, the car was locked — and my keys were still inside it!"

"Oh, dear," said Rupert. "How are you going to get in?"

"I'm on my way to the locksmith now," said the doctor. "He'll help. I don't know how the door locked itself. It's a mystery!"

At the corner, Rupert said goodbye to Doctor Lion and carried on towards the general store. He decided to call in on Mrs Trunk on the way to find out how his friend was feeling.

It was a fine morning and the air was full of birdsong, but as Rupert came closer to the Trunks' house, he noticed another sound: a horrible banging and thumping.

Across the road was Doctor Lion's car, still parked where he had left it the night before. Rupert went to have a look at it. The banging seemed to come from inside the car. He peered through the window — and had quite a shock.

Glaring out at him was an angry face!

"You!" came a fierce little voice. "I might have known it was you! Let me out!"

"Raggety!" cried Rupert. "What are you doing in Doctor Lion's car?"

"Let me out first," said Raggety angrily. "Then you can tell me why you shut me in this stupid box!"

"But I didn't!" cried Rupert.

Raggety took no notice of Rupert. He just kept on banging and screaming, "Let me out!" at the top of his shrill voice.

"Listen, Raggety," said Rupert. "If you stop banging and shouting, I'll help you to get out."

"Hurry up," said Raggety crossly.

Rupert told Raggety how to unlock the car door from the inside.

"A likely story," said Raggety, as he reached for the door handle.

The old car door creaked open and Raggety climbed out.

He yawned, stretched and then turned to Rupert with a frown.

"So I could have escaped from that nasty trap last night, could I?" he asked.

"It's not a trap," said Rupert. "It's Doctor Lion's car. Why were you in it, anyway?"

"It was very cold last night," complained Raggety. "I climbed in to warm myself up and shut the door to keep out the draughts."

"You must have locked the door by mistake," said Rupert. "But didn't you hear Doctor Lion trying to open the door?"

"It was so lovely and snug in there that I ell asleep. The next thing I heard was the lawn chorus," said Raggety. "I've been rapped in that horrible thing for ages! I lon't want to see another car ever again!"

Rupert watched as Raggety stomped off across Nutwood Common.

Rupert looked inside the car again, and spotted the doctor's keys. He picked them up, shut the door and locked it. Then he carefully crossed the road and ran towards the shops. If he was quick, he could catch Doctor Lion at the locksmith's.

Rupert dashed into the locksmith's shop and handed the doctor his keys. He didn't notice a small piece of paper falling out of his pocket onto the locksmith's floor.

"Thank you, Rupert," said Doctor Lion. "You're just in time! But how did you get my keys out of the car?"

Rupert told him all about Raggety's night in the cosy car.

"I was only passing your car because I wanted to see how Edward was feeling," he explained.

"Edward's fine now," said Doctor Lion.

"I'm glad he's better," said Rupert. Then he remembered why he had walked into Nutwood. "Oh, no!" he cried. "I haven't done the shopping!"

After Rupert had left the shop, the locksmith pointed to something on the floor. “Look! What’s that?”

Doctor Lion picked up the piece of paper and read it carefully.

"Hey, Rupert!"

Rupert was on his way to Mrs Fox's shop when he heard someone calling him.

"Hello, Bill! Hello, Algy!" He turned and greeted his friends.

"We're going round to see how Edward's feeling," said Bill. "His mother had to call the doctor last night."

"I know," said Rupert. "You'll never guess what happened to Doctor Lion's car while he was in the Trunks' house."

Bill and Algy listened intently while Rupert told them the whole story. None of them noticed Doctor Lion walk quietly by on the other side of the road.

"So you didn't go to see Edward after all," said Algy.

"Why don't you come with us now?" asked Bill.

"I'm afraid I'll have to see him later," replied Rupert. "I'm just going for some shopping for my mother."

Rupert waved goodbye to his friends and walked down the street and into the general store.

"Good morning, Rupert," said Mrs Fox. "What can I do for you today?"

"Hello, Mrs Fox. My mother needs some extra provisions," said Rupert. "She's given me a shopping list."

Rupert put his hand in his pocket and pulled out — nothing! He tried the other pocket. It was empty, too. He had lost the shopping list!

Mrs Fox looked concerned. "Have you lost something, Rupert?" she asked.

Before Rupert could reply, Mrs Fox put a bag full of groceries on the counter.

"It's all right, Rupert," she said. "Doctor Lion found your shopping list on the locksmith's floor and brought it straight round to me. I've already packed your shopping for you!"

Rupert thanked Mrs Fox and walked home as quickly as he could.

Mrs Bear was in the kitchen.

"Let's see what you've brought for me," she said, unpacking the shopping bag. "Eggs, tomatoes, carrots — what's this?"

Mrs Bear took out a packet of biscuits and handed them to Rupert.

"They're my favourites!" said Rupert.

"I know," said Mrs Bear. "Thank you for doing the shopping, Rupert. And you were so quick, too!"

RUPERT